Steven Brantley

Judi Brantley

Presented To:

Natalie

— With Love —

By:

Grandpa & Grandma Gratsch

On:

Christmas 2001

To the Heavenly Father

for His providence and provision for us

—and for Pearl.

T.S.B. & J.S.B.

For my Mother and Iva.

D.L.H.

A LETTER FROM PEARL

The story you are about to experience was written for children of all ages to teach the need and importance of personal and spiritual relationships.

Woven throughout, like threads of gold, is God's enduring love for all and softly conveyed is, "We love because he first loved us."(NIV).

My story is one of redemption and adoption, reflective of the redemption and adoption Our Great Shepherd, Jesus, offers. After being appraised as only a throwaway, I am found, tended to, and adopted, because no one is a throwaway in the eyes of God.

Within these pages Monty and I learn to live out the first and second great commandments, "Love the Lord your God with all your heart..." and "Love your neighbor as yourself."(NIV).

Finally, you will see Owl, in his role as vicar to the animals, fulfill the great commission, "Go ye into all the world, and preach the gospel to every creature."(KJV).

I hope you will enjoy this timeless little tale, discover new treasures from within, and with every reading feel close to the heart of God, for that is indeed where we all live.

Pearl

The Throwaway Cat

Steven & Judi Brantley

Illustrated by Del Holt

Spring House Books

Wadmalaw Island, South Carolina

Pearl sat on the window sill, warming herself in the sun and waiting for Monty. Every morning he came scampering by, as squirrels do, stopping occasionally for a chat. She didn't want to appear too eager because she was quite a lady kitten, but, without realizing it, she had grown very fond of their morning meetings. And this morning he was late.

The other animals must miss him, too. She heard Francine sounding off, as a French Toulouse goose is prone to do, "Have you seen Master Monty—Mayor of the Manor— this morning?"

Pearl was too young to understand what was meant when she heard them say, "He's like a mayor all right. He loves to be in everybody's business."

It seemed to Pearl that Monty knew just about everything about everyone in the country. And although he always appeared very nervous, she thought he was genuine in his concern about the welfare of all the animals.

Only yesterday, she was telling a group of jays her feelings about him. They had laughed and said, "Just wait—you'll learn."

Sitting higher up in the tree, with his eyes closed—partially—
Owl, of the British Barn sort, appeared absolutely uninterested in
their conversation, but heard it all.

Pearl looked up to Owl. Maybe she was too young to understand everything about life. And maybe she did have a lot to learn. But as she studied Owl, she became very sure of something: He was wise. He didn't talk much, mostly he just listened.

From somewhere deep within, Pearl began to feel that Owl knew secrets. She wondered if he would be willing to share them and she was determined to find out. And somehow, she knew the right time to ask him would come.

While waiting for Monty, Pearl had preened and primped past the point of perfection. And now, leaning over the window sill, stretching her neck and small face forward to look farther down the yard, she saw him coming. She pulled back quickly, stretched nonchalantly and yawned.

As nervous as always, he greeted her. "Oh my! Good morning, Miss Pearl. I'm sorry if I made you wait and perhaps worry.
I was in attendance at the birth of the new baby," Monty explained,
quite out of breath.

"New baby?"

Yes," he said, scratching behind his ear. "Dominique's due date was days ago. This is her first fawn and we were worried. But our fears were unfounded—her fawn is fine," Monty said exaggerating his English accent. "And how are you, this glorious good day?"

"Very well—thank you for asking. Why were you in attendance at the fawn's birth?" Pearl asked, puzzled by his accounting.

"Oh, well, you know records must be kept and I *am* the appointed record keeper. The care of the animals has fallen my lot. Which brings us to a repeated point and query. I don't have the record of your coming. I must have that! When will be a good time for us to discuss it for the record, Miss Pearl?" he politely asked.

She liked him! She didn't see in him the things the others saw. With the weight of the animal world on his shoulders—and she had no idea how big that was—she now knew why he always acted so nervous. He said he was the appointed caretaker of the animals. *Who appointed him?* she wondered. She would ask Owl. She knew that Owl, as wise as he was, would know.

Answering Monty as a proper lady kitten would, Pearl said, "Well, I suppose this morning will work."

Pearl had put off telling him her story because part of it was too scary to recall and repeat. But the other part was so perfectly pleasant, and she was so proud of her new family, the Lord and Lady with whom she now lived, she must make it a part of the record.

Monty started scrambling. Getting his pencil and stenopad, he was ready to record. "At your service, Miss Pearl."

"Just a minute, Monty," Pearl said politely.

Leaving her window sill, she ran to the library and jumped up into the lap of her Lord. He stroked her softly as he read the morning paper and said something Pearl didn't understand. Actually, she didn't understand any of the noises her Lord and Lady made—except one—well, perhaps—two. She understood "NO!" and "DOWN!" and thinking for a moment, she knew two more—making four—"PEARL!" "COME!"

After getting her Lord's attention, she ran to the door where she sat in the sun, longingly looking out. He continued to read his paper. Pearl stretched. Then, she pressed her paws on the glass door. She looked out again, looked at him and said, "Please sir—may I go out?" which sounded like, "Pr-r-r-r-r-ow! P-r-r-r-ow! Yck-yck-yck?" to him. But he understood! He came and opened the door.

She quickly ran out. The elegant English countryside was dressed in Spring.

The lilacs, lilies, and lady-slippers, arrayed in their finest as if they were awaiting an invitation to afternoon tea, lined the walk. Stopping along the way to smell the beauty Spring brought, she slowly made her way to Monty. This was her first spring. Pearl didn't know people called what she was feeling "spring fever." She just knew she was in love with life and her Lord and Lady, of course.

Approaching the tree where Monty waited, appearing quite official, she stopped. He wasn't one for missing details. "Miss Pearl, you're trembling. Is your story that terrible?"

"It wouldn't have been for you," she said recalling her flight through the air. "But it certainly was for me."

"Oh, my! I am sorry to put you through this. Perhaps—"

"No, Monty, really I'll be fine. It's only the first part that's scary."

"Well, if you're sure."

I was only a few weeks old," she began, "four weeks, I guess. We were all nuzzling with Mummy—we thought we were hidden. Suddenly, we heard a thunderous sound. It was terrible. I had just gotten my eyes open when I saw it coming. My Mummy started screaming and scratching and biting and bucking. A huge hand grabbed me and dropped me into a box. And right on top of me came my sister, my brother, the twins and finally Mummy.

Immediately it got dark—too dark to see exactly what was happening. But in a few minutes, the box landed with a big thud. Next I heard another scary noise. I didn't know what it was, then, but now I know it was the truck engine.

"Before long the box began bumping up and down and that hand kept coming in—over and over. I was bewildered and after a bit, I realized I was in the box by myself and that huge hand came in one more time—for me!

And then, the wind was fierce! I was flying through the air! I was thrown away! But when I began to fall, it seemed like a wondrous wing slipped under me, and I slid safely to the ground.

"It was as if Someone was watching over me and taking care of me, because I barely bumped my nose. But it did bleed, just a little.

I was stunned. I scrambled into the grass and sat crying—unable to imagine what I had done to deserve such fright.

"Within minutes I saw another huge hand coming—I cowered down in the brambles—but this one was different. For all the hurt, the first hand brought—this hand brought healing.

Ever so gently he picked me up. He held me close to his heart—I heard it beating. He carried me home, and tended my wounds. And I have lived happily hereafter, with my Lord and Lady."

B-B-But, w-w-who was w-w-watching over y-y-you? It w-w-wasn't m-m-me," Monty stuttered, growing evermore nervous, and feeling a failure as the appointed caretaker of the animals.

"I don't know," Pearl said. "Someone surely was. Let's ask Owl, he'll know. He's very wise."

Monty seemed to fly through the air, as he leaped from limb to limb, looking for Owl. Pearl, barely able to keep up, as she raced by leaps and bounds on the ground, heard him holler, "Here he is!"

Climbing up to where Monty and Owl were waiting, Pearl explained, "Owl, excuse us for waking you but we have a very important query."

Blinking his big eyes awake he said, "But, of course—no bother a'tall. Who will ask the query?"

"Me! I will. It's about me," said Pearl. "Who was watching over me on the day I was thrown away? Monty says he's the appointed caretaker of the animals, but he wasn't there. It wasn't him. Someone must have seen me safely through it and sent that wondrous wing I slid down."

Nodding his head and heart-shaped face slowly, with the voice of a vicar, Owl said, "Yes, Someone did—the King of Kings—the Lord of Lords—Our Creator. And being Lord of all creation, He's the One who provided the Lord and Lady with whom you now live."

"Are you talking about God?" Monty asked, but without giving Owl a chance to answer, continued. "Surely, as wise as you are you don't believe in something you can't even see? Besides, everyone knows I *am* the appointed caretaker of the animals."

"Monty, ole chap, sorry to be so blunt, but you can't even begin to imagine how immense the animal world is, much less take care of it. And it was you who assumed that great task you're always talking about—not *seeing* anyone else fulfilling it. Just because you can't see God doesn't mean He isn't there, watching over us all, every minute of every day. You believe in the wind, do you not?" Owl asked.

Of course I do! I don't have to see the wind. I can feel it!" Monty said, a bit sarcastically.

"You can feel God, too!"

"Where—how?" Monty was curious.

"Right now—by telling Him you accept Him, as the appointed caretaker of us all."

"I can do that," Monty said nonchalantly, "But how will that make me feel Him?"

"If you are earnest, accept Him and see," Owl coaxed.

Looking higher than the trees, Monty said aloud, "God, Owl's right. I haven't believed in You, because I can't see You. He says I can feel You though and that's fine by me—that's what I need. I do, with all my heart, accept You."

Watching Monty closely, Pearl saw him appear to lose his balance—she gasped—he almost fell off the limb!

"Wh-wh-what happened?" he said holding on, "Something h-h-happened to m-m-my b-b-back. I feel light as a bird feather." Swishing his bushy tail back and forth, standing on his haunches, "Owl!" Monty demanded, "What happened?"

"Monty, you feel the gift of God! The burden that you assumed for care of the animal world has been lifted. It was never yours to carry! Let Him be the caretaker and you continue to be the record keeper. God is real! He created us all! He loves us and is watching over us! Enjoy life! Have fun! Honor Him!"

Quietly, without query, looking higher than the trees, Pearl said, "With all my heart, I accept you, too. And I thank You kindly, for my Lord and Lady."

"Any other queries?" Owl asked.

Pearl and Monty looked at each other, shook their heads, and together said, "Not today, Owl. We thank you."

Pearl had known that Owl knew a secret. She knew the right time would come for her to know it, too. Today had been the right time. And she was ever so thankful that she and her friend Monty shared it.

Laughing and rejoicing, they chased each other down the tree and joined the whole earth singing in harmony, "For the beauty of the earth, For the glory of the skies...Lord of all to Thee we raise, This our hymn of grateful praise. Amen."

PEARL'S PET VERSES

For every animal of the forest is mine, and the cattle on a thousand hills. I know every bird in the mountains, and the creatures of the field are mine. (Psalm 50:10-11, NIV).

Consider the ravens: They do not sow or reap, they have no storeroom or barn; yet God feeds them. (Luke 12:24, NIV).

The Lord protects the simplehearted; when I was in great need, he saved me.   (Psalm 116:6, NIV).

Trust in the Lord with all your heart and lean not on your own understanding.   (Proverbs 3:5, NIV).

And be ye kind one to another. . . (Ephesians 4:32, KJV).

And we know that all things work together for good to them that love God. . .   (Romans 8:28, KJV).

". . . Love the Lord your God with all your heart and with all your soul and with all your mind . . . Love your neighbor as yourself." (Matthew 22:37-39, NIV).

". . .Go ye into all the world, and preach the gospel to every creature." (Mark 16:15, KJV).

This is the day the Lord has made, let us rejoice and be glad in it. (Psalm 118:24, NIV).

GLOSSARY

BEWILDERED: to be confused about things that are happening.

GENUINE: the real thing; sincere.

IMMENSE: huge; extremely large.

LADY: a British title given to women of certain rank.

LORD: a British title given to men of certain rank.

LOT: one's fortune in life; the deciding of a matter by chance.

MANOR: an English estate or property.

NUZZLING: to nestle; snuggle.

PREENED: to clean and groom.

QUERY: to inquire; question.

SPRING FEVER: the excitement one may feel as spring arrives.

UNFOUNDED: not based on fact or truth.

VICAR: a minister for the churches in England.

ACKNOWLEDGMENTS

The authors and publisher wish to thank all those who gave editorial advice for the clarity and correctness of this text: Sally E. Stuart, Larry Carlson, Joan Shifflette, Melissa Shifflette, and Margaret McIntosh. Without their efforts this book would not be what it is.

Published by Spring House Books
Wadmalaw Island, South Carolina

FIRST EDITION

Scripture quotations marked (NIV) are from the HOLY BIBLE, NEW INTERNATIONAL VERSION®. NIV® Copyright© 1973, 1978, 1984 by International Bible Society. All rights reserved. All other scripture quoted is from THE HOLY BIBLE, The Authorized King James Version and marked (KJV).

Typesetting and Formatting by Jon Verdi and The Summerhouse Press
Printed and Bound in Hong Kong by C & C Offset Printing Company LTD

Library of Congress Catalog Number 98-90767

ISBN 1-892570-00-9

10 9 8 7 6 5 4 3 2 1

ABOUT
SPRING HOUSE BOOKS

Here at Spring House Books we are very pleased to offer, *THE THROW-AWAY CAT*, the first in our list of Christian Children's storybooks. What you will find in this book and our storybooks that follow are "everyday images of God." Because we believe, —"in him we live and move and have our being"— the storybooks we publish will set forth examples for children to see God's loving hand in the everyday events of their lives.

When Jesus was asked who was greatest in the kingdom of heaven, He said that little children and those who believe and become like little children are the greatest in the kingdom of heaven. So while our storybooks are expressly written for children of chronological age, they will most certainly bear a message to the hearts of children of all ages.

Spring House Books is committed to promoting Christian values through education and entertainment and to that end we are making this book, as well as our future storybooks, available for fund raising, at special discounts, for schools, churches and charitable organizations. For more information please contact us at:

SPRING HOUSE BOOKS
P.O. Box 129
Wadmalaw Island, SC 29487
(843) 559-9307 fax# (843) 559-4759
For individual orders you may call our toll-free ordering line:
1-877-559-4759

Authors' Post Script: Reading to and with children can create a safe and secure place for dialogue. We think you have an excellent tool for that in *The Throwaway Cat,* because many questions may spring forth that are unanswered. By leaving unanswered questions, you exercise your own creativity and encourage children to do likewise.